NICOLA KINNEAR

A little bit BRAVE

Orchard Books • New York
An Imprint of Scholastic Inc.

Logan was a stay-at-home bunny.
His friend Luna was the daring one.
She had new adventures every day.
They sounded quite exciting, but
rather frightening, too.

So whenever Luna said: "Come out with me! It's fun!"

Logan said, "Oh, no.
I'll never go outside. It's far too scary."

At last, Luna had had enough.
"You have to come out with me!"

"No!"
said Logan.

"You're no fun!"
said Luna.

"I'm too scared!"
said Logan.

"Sometimes, Logan, you just have to be a little bit brave!" shouted Luna.

And she stomped out.

Logan tried to have
a normal morning.

He watered his
indoor plants.

He dusted his shell collection.

He baked some cookies. But nothing felt right. He was very upset. Luna had never been angry with him before.

"I have to make it up with her right away," he thought. There was just one problem. Luna was . . .

OUTSIDE!

It would be an adventure, and Logan had never had one of those. He had no idea what to pack, so he took a snorkel, a flashlight, and a tin of cookies.

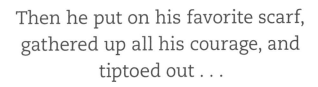

Then he put on his favorite scarf, gathered up all his courage, and tiptoed out . . .

It was strange and noisy in the woods.
There was flapping and scurrying,
tweeting and rustling.

"I knew it would be scary,"
thought Logan.

He took a deep breath
and called:

"LUNA!!!"

There was no reply . . .

. . . but lots of other
animals scampered up.
"Luna?" they said. "She's the
bravest bunny in the world."

"She dives into the river
to collect shells,"
said an otter.

"She rides around the
forest on my back," said a deer.

"She explores the deep, dark caves
and goes looking for bears,"
said a fox.

"That sounds so scary!"
said Logan.

"But if you do those things, too,"
said a mouse, "perhaps you'll find her."
So that's exactly what Logan did.

First he dived into the river —

SPLASH!

Brr! It was chilly!
It was lucky he'd
packed his snorkel.

There was a whole new
world underwater. Logan saw
fish and frogs and snails.

But he didn't see Luna.

Then he rode off with the deer —

WHOOSH!

My, it was fast! It was lucky he'd brought his scarf,
to help him hold on. There was a whole new world in
the woods. He saw sparrows and squirrels and butterflies.

But he didn't see Luna.

Then he
tiptoed into
a cave —

EEK!

It was lucky he'd packed his flashlight.
There was a whole new world in the dark.
He saw bats and spiders and sleeping bears.

But he didn't see Luna.

Logan was amazed at all the things he'd done.
"If only I could find Luna!" he said.
"She'd be really proud of me."
He was so pleased with himself,
he decided to have a cookie.

But before he could open the tin, he heard a shout:

"STAY BACK, YOU WICKED WOLF!"

That voice sounded very familiar.
In fact, it sounded just like . . .

. . . Luna!
Oh, no! A huge,
hungry wolf was
trying to eat her!

Logan hid behind a tree.
Suddenly he didn't feel brave at all.
"I want to go home!" he whimpered.

But he couldn't let Luna be eaten.
So he picked up his cookies, gathered
up all his courage . . .

. . . and ran!

"NOoooooo o o o o o O!!!"

he cried.
"Don't eat Luna!"

"Eat my cookies!"

The wolf was
very surprised.

"Cookies?" he said.
"I don't mind if I do!"
And he gobbled up
the whole lot.

The wolf was very friendly after that.
"That was amazing!" cried Luna.
"When did you become
so brave?"

"I think it started this morning," said Logan,
"when I was baking cookies."

Luna laughed. "Shall we go home and bake some more?"

"I'd like that," said Logan. "But first . . .

"... we need another adventure!"

ISBN 978-1-338-56327-6

10 9 8 7 6 5 4 3 2 1   20 21 22 23 24

Printed in Malaysia   108

This edition first printing, April 2020

For Andrew

Thank you to Zoë, Alison and Helen for all your help and support.

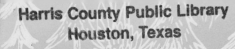

2